Put Beginning Readers on the Right Track with
ALL ABOARD READING™

Picture Readers—for Ages 3 to 6
Picture Readers have super-simple texts, with many nouns appearing as rebus pictures. At the end of each book are 24 flash cards—on one side is the rebus picture; on the other side is the written-out word.

Pre-Level 1—for Ages 4 to 6
First Friends, First Readers have a super-simple text starring lovable recurring characters. Each book features two easy stories that will hold the attention of even the youngest reader while promoting an early sense of accomplishment.

Level 1—for Preschool through First-Grade Children
Level 1 books have very few lines per page, very large type, easy words, lots of repetition, and pictures with visual "cues" to help children figure out the words on the page.

Level 2—for First-Grade to Third-Grade Children
Level 2 books are printed in slightly smaller type than Level 1 books. The stories are more complex, but there is still lots of repetition in the text, and many pictures. The sentences are quite simple and are broken up into short lines to make reading easier.

Level 3—for Second-Grade through Third-Grade Children
Level 3 books have considerably longer texts, harder words, and more complicated sentences.

All Aboard for happy reading!

For Sherry Litwack, who rivals
Moffie and Sally in the "Fashion World,"
Fraser and Alexander, and, of course, Mario.

Jennifer Smith-Stead, Literacy Consultant

Library of Congress Cataloging-in-Publication Data is available.

ISBN 0-448-42617-X (GB)   A   B   C   D   E   F   G   H   I   J
ISBN 0-448-42545-9 (pbk.)   A   B   C   D   E   F   G   H   I   J

HIDE-AND-SEEK
ALL WEEK

by Tomie dePaola

Grosset & Dunlap • New York

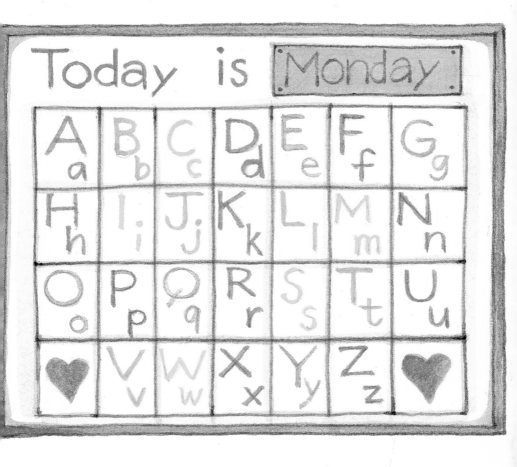

All the kids in kindergarten
were writing their names.
Moffie wrote M-O-F-F-A-T.
Morgie wrote M-O-R-G-A-N.
"Good job!" Ms. Shepherd
told the twins.

RING!

"There is the bell for recess,"
Ms. Shepherd said.
"Class, you have worked hard.
Now it is time to play."

Everyone ran out
to the playground.
"Let's play Hide-and-Seek,"
Morgie said to Billy.

Moffie and Sally wanted to play.

"I will be IT," Moffie said.

But Morgie shook his head.

"We have to pick who will be IT."

Morgie wanted to toss a coin.

Sally wanted
to do One Potato, Two Potato.

Billy wanted to go by the ABCs

because "Billy" began with a B.

"I have the most gold stars,"
   Moffie said.

"So I should be IT!"

"I have gold stars, too," Sally said.

"Let's ask Ms. Shepherd,"
   Billy said.

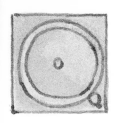

RING!

Recess was over.

"We will have to wait until tomorrow," Morgie said.

There was the bell for recess.

"Class, put away your crayons
and your maps," Ms. Shepherd said.

13

The four friends got ready
to play Hide-and-Seek.
"We can decide who is IT later,"
Moffie said.
"Now we need rules about hiding."

"I will make a map,"
Sally said.

"The swings are

out-of-bounds," Billy said.

"The tubes are too easy,"

Moffie said.

"The tree is too tall," Sally said.

"I don't like to climb."

Recess was over.

"We will have to wait

until tomorrow," Billy said.

"Good," Ms. Shepherd said,

"Now everyone can count to ten."

 RING!

There was the bell for recess.

The four friends met by the slide.

"We forgot Counting Rules,"
Moffie said.

"I can count to twenty,"
Sally said.

"I can only count to ten,"
 Morgie said.

"You can count to ten <u>two</u> times,"
 Billy said.

"Ten and ten make twenty."

"Okay!" Morgie said.

"But you are not IT," Moffie said.

"And we still don't have a map."

"We will have to wait
    until tomorrow," Sally said.

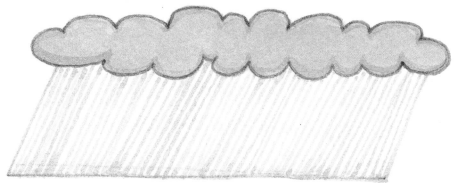

The next day it was raining.

"We must stay inside today,"

Ms. Shepherd said.

They went to the gym for recess.
"Well," Moffie said,
"we can't play Hide-and-Seek
in here!"

The class played
Duck, Duck, Goose.
Everyone knew the rules for that!

"Hand in hand, Hansel and Gretel

ran all the way home,"

Ms. Shepherd read.

"The end."

Ms. Shepherd closed the book.

 RING!

It was recess.

"We can't play Hide-and-Seek yet.
We need to pick Home Base,"
Moffie said.

"Home can be the tree,"
Morgie said.

"I don't like the tree," Sally said.

"Home can be the school wall."

"No," Billy said.

"Home can be the slide."

No one could decide.

"Let's forget about
   Hide-and-Seek," Morgie said.
"Let's play Steal the Bacon.
   We can get some more
   kids to play."

"First we have to make the rules,"
Billy said.

Everybody nodded.

"But this time we need <u>rules</u>
for making the rules,"
Sally said.

"I will do that," Moffie said.
"I will have them ready
for Monday!"